THE CHRISTMAS TREE BOOK

by Carol North
illustrated by Diane Dawson

MERRIGOLD PRESS • NEW YORK

ISBN: 0-307-11173-3

It's nearly Christmas—
time to get a Christmas tree.

Father Bear and the Baby Bears
are going into town to buy a tree.

"I think that one will do just fine," says Father Bear.

Father Bear ties the tree to the car. The Baby Bears help.

When they get home, Father Bear saws off the bottom of the tree so it will fit into the tree stand.

Mamma Bear waters the tree to keep it moist.

"Now where are the decorations from last year?" Mamma Bear says as she pokes through boxes in the attic.

“Here’s the star I made when I was a little bear,” says Sister Bear.

Grandma Bear helps the Baby Bears make stars and paper chains.

Grandpa Bear and Sister Bear put the lights on the tree.

Then the Baby Bears put on popcorn strings and the paper chains.

The tree is almost finished. There are red and gold balls, little wooden horses, lots of candy canes, and even a Santa in a sleigh.

Sister Bear puts her star on the very top of the tree. Now it *is* finished.

Father Bear serves hot chocolate and they all sit down to look at the tree. Everyone feels tired and happy.

“Listen to the carolers outside,” says Grandma Bear.
“What a nice time we’ve had today,” says Mamma Bear.

Everyone goes upstairs to bed.

The Baby Bears dream about Santa coming.

He does come!

"This is the prettiest tree I've seen yet," says Santa Bear.

In the morning, the Baby Bears run downstairs and find the tricycles Santa has left for them. They are pleased indeed. "This is the best Christmas ever," they say.